The Gingerbread Man

Adapted by DONNA R. PARNELL
Illustrated by JEAN CHANDLER

Ladybird Books

LADYBIRD BOOKS, INC.
Auburn, Maine 04210 U.S.A.
© LADYBIRD BOOKS LTD MCMLXXXVII
Loughborough, Leicestershire, England

Printed in U.S.A.

A little old woman
and a little old man
lived in a little old house.

One day, the little old woman said,
"I will make something good to eat."

So she made a gingerbread man,
and put him in the oven to bake.

After a while,
the little old woman said,
"That gingerbread man
must be ready now."

She opened the oven door.
Out popped the gingerbread man.

The gingerbread man
ran across the room.
He ran out the door.

"Stop!" cried the little old woman.
"Stop!" cried the little old man.

But the gingerbread man
did not stop.

He said,
"Run, run, as fast as you can.
You can't catch me,
I'm the gingerbread man!"

The gingerbread man
ran past a cat.
''Stop!'' said the cat.
''I want to eat you.''

"No," said the gingerbread man.
"Run, run, as fast as you can.
You can't catch me,
I'm the gingerbread man!"

The gingerbread man
ran past a cow.
"Stop!" said the cow.
"I want to eat you."

"No," said the gingerbread man.
"Run, run, as fast as you can.
You can't catch me,
I'm the gingerbread man!"

The gingerbread man
ran past a fox.
"Stop!" said the fox.

"No," said the gingerbread man.
"Run, run, as fast as you can.
You can't catch me,
I'm the gingerbread man!"

The gingerbread man
came to a river.
"I can't swim," he said.
"How will I get across?"

The fox said, "I will help you.
Jump onto my tail."

The gingerbread man
jumped onto the fox's tail.
Soon the fox said,
"You will get wet.
Jump onto my back."

The gingerbread man
jumped onto the fox's back.

Soon the fox said,
"You will get wet.
Jump onto my head."
The gingerbread man
jumped onto the fox's head.

Then the fox said,
"You will get wet.
Jump onto my nose."
The gingerbread man
jumped onto the fox's nose.

The fox opened his mouth wide,
and ate up the gingerbread man.

And that was the end
of the gingerbread man!